THIS BOOK BELONGS TO

____

FOR THE KIDS WHO LOVE MAGIC

ISBN: 9798894581903

ELLIOT'S CAULDRON BUBBLED AS HE STIRRED THE SHIMMERING BLUE LIQUID. POTION-MAKING WAS HIS FAVORITE CLASS, THOUGH CHARLOTTE, HIS RIVAL, ALWAYS ACTED LIKE SHE KNEW BETTER.

SUDDENLY, A LOUD CRASH! ECHOED FROM THE ALCHEMY LAB NEXT DOOR. ELLIOT EXCHANGED GLANCES WITH FELIX, HIS MISCHIEVOUS BLACK CAT COMPANION. "WHAT WAS THAT?"

WHEN ELLIOT ARRIVED, SHARDS OF GLASS COVERED THE FLOOR. SHELVES WERE EMPTIED OF RARE POTIONS—IRREPLACEABLE INGREDIENTS GONE. A GRIM MESSAGE WAS SCRAWLED IN FROST ACROSS THE WALL: "FIND ME IF YOU DARE."

THE HEADMISTRESS, STERN AND IMPOSING, ADDRESSED THE STUDENTS THE NEXT MORNING. "A THIEF IS AMONG US. UNTIL THEY ARE CAUGHT, POTION-MAKING IS SUSPENDED." GASPS FILLED THE ROOM.

DETERMINED TO SOLVE THE MYSTERY, ELLIOT INVESTIGATED THE LAB WITH FELIX. BENEATH A SHELF, HE FOUND A STRANGE FUR FRAGMENT SHIMMERING FAINTLY IN THE LIGHT.

MAX, HIS OWL COMPANION, SWOOPED DOWN WITH A LETTER CLUTCHED IN HIS TALONS. THE NOTE READ: "THE WOODS HOLD ANSWERS." ELLIOT'S HEART RACED.

ELLIOT BEGAN LISTING SUSPECTS. CHARLOTTE, THE PERFECTIONIST, HAD EVERYTHING TO GAIN FROM STEALING RARE POTIONS. LYLE, THE PREFECT, HAD BEEN SNEAKING AROUND. THEO, HIS ROOMMATE, HAD GROWN SECRETIVE.

HE COULDN'T RULE OUT GREGOR, THE GROUNDSKEEPER WITH A DARK PAST, OR IRIS, THE BRILLIANT BUT RECLUSIVE ALCHEMIST. THE FUR, HOWEVER, SUGGESTED SOMETHING MORE THAN HUMAN.

THE TREES GREW DARKER, THE AIR COLDER. SUDDENLY, GROWLS SURROUNDED THEM. WOLVES WITH ICY BLUE EYES EMERGED FROM THE SHADOWS, BLOCKING THEIR PATH.

THE LARGEST WOLF SNARLED, ITS FANGS GLINTING. ELLIOT CLUTCHED HIS WAND. "I'M NOT AFRAID!" HE SHOUTED, THOUGH HIS KNEES SHOOK.

THE WOLVES LUNGED. ELLIOT RAISED A SHIMMERING SHIELD SPELL.
THE IMPACT SENT SPARKS FLYING, BUT THE WOLVES KEPT CIRCLING.

FELIX LEAPED ONTO A WOLF'S BACK, CLAWING AT ITS ICY FUR. MAX SWOOPED DOWN, PECKING ANOTHER'S EARS. ELLIOT USED A FIRE SPELL, FORCING THE WOLVES TO RETREAT.

ONE WOLF, WOUNDED BUT DEFIANT, WHISPERED, "YOU SEEK THE THIEF,
BUT BEWARE... ONE OF YOUR OWN CANNOT BE TRUSTED."
THEN IT VANISHED INTO THE SHADOWS.

SHAKEN, ELLIOT PRESSED ON. HE FOUND A FORGOTTEN MAP HIDDEN UNDER A ROCK.
IT SHOWED A PATH LEADING TO AN ANCIENT VAULT BENEATH THE SCHOOL.

BACK AT SCHOOL, ELLIOT SHARED HIS SUSPICIONS WITH HIS FRIENDS. "ONE OF THE SUSPECTS IS BEHIND THIS," HE INSISTED. "BUT WHO?"

CHARLOTTE SNEERED WHEN ELLIOT QUESTIONED HER. "ME? STEAL POTIONS? UNLIKE YOU, I DON'T NEED TO CHEAT TO WIN!" SHE HUFFED.

ELLIOT FOUND LYLE IN THE PREFECT'S TOWER. "I'VE SEEN YOU SNEAKING AROUND," HE ACCUSED. LYLE'S EYES NARROWED. "YOU'D BETTER MIND YOUR OWN BUSINESS."

IRIS ADMITTED SHE'D BEEN STUDYING RARE POTIONS BUT DENIED STEALING THEM. "WHOEVER DID THIS IS AFTER MORE THAN INGREDIENTS," SHE WHISPERED.

GREGOR, MEANWHILE, LAUGHED AT ELLIOT'S ACCUSATIONS. "A THIEF? ME? YOU'VE BEEN READING TOO MANY FAIRY TALES, BOY."

THE SCHOOL LIBRARY WAS ELLIOT'S NEXT STOP. DEEP WITHIN ITS TOWERING SHELVES, HE UNCOVERED A BOOK ON MAGICAL CREATURES. FLIPPING THROUGH THE PAGES, HE STOPPED AT AN ILLUSTRATION OF WOLVES WITH ICY BLUE EYES. "THE FROST WOLVES," HE MUTTERED. "GUARDIANS OF SECRETS, BUT EASILY SWAYED BY TRICKERY."

THE BOOK MENTIONED A MYSTERIOUS CAVE IN THE DARKWOOD FOREST WHERE FROST WOLVES GATHERED. IT WAS SAID TO HOLD AN ANCIENT VAULT TIED TO THE SCHOOL'S OLDEST MAGIC. ELLIOT SCRIBBLED THE LOCATION ON A SCRAP OF PARCHMENT.

THAT NIGHT, FELIX PAWED AT ELLIOT'S FACE, WAKING HIM. MAX HOOTED SOFTLY FROM THE WINDOW, SIGNALING SOMEONE WAS OUTSIDE. CLUTCHING HIS WAND, ELLIOT FOLLOWED THEM INTO THE CHILLY NIGHT.

THEO WAS SLIPPING INTO THE WOODS. HIS WAND GLOWED FAINTLY, ILLUMINATING A PATH. "WHAT'S HE UP TO?" ELLIOT WHISPERED, KEEPING HIS DISTANCE.

SUDDENLY, THEO DISAPPEARED INTO THE SHADOWS. ELLIOT TURNED TO FELIX. "WE NEED TO KNOW WHAT HE'S HIDING." MAX FLAPPED ABOVE, GUIDING THEM TOWARD THE PATH THEO HAD TAKEN.

THE FOREST GREW DARKER, THE AIR COLDER. WEBS SHIMMERED IN THE MOONLIGHT. "SPIDERS," ELLIOT WHISPERED, STEPPING CAREFULLY.

A RUSTLING SOUND FROZE ELLIOT IN PLACE. MASSIVE SPIDERS EMERGED, THEIR GLOWING EYES FIXATED ON HIM. FELIX HISSED AND DARTED FORWARD, CLAWING AT THE CLOSEST ONE.

ELLIOT CAST A SPELL, A BURST OF LIGHT SCATTERING THE SPIDERS. THEY RETREATED INTO THE SHADOWS, BUT ONE REMAINED. IT WHISPERED IN A VOICE LIKE CRACKING ICE: "THE THIEF SEEKS THE ELIXIR OF DOMINION. BEWARE WHO YOU TRUST."

BEFORE ELLIOT COULD ASK MORE, THE SPIDER DISSOLVED INTO GLITTERING DUST. "ELIXIR OF DOMINION?" HE MUTTERED, HIS MIND RACING.

RETURNING TO THE SCHOOL, ELLIOT SNUCK BACK INTO THE DORMITORY JUST AS DAWN BROKE. HE BARELY HAD TIME TO REST BEFORE CHARLOTTE STORMED INTO THE COMMON ROOM. "YOU LOOK AWFUL," SHE SAID WITH A SMIRK.

Ignoring her, Elliot asked, "What do you know about the Elixir of Dominion?" Charlotte's eyes widened, but she quickly hid her surprise. "It's a myth," she said. "Why do you ask?"

ELLIOT WATCHED HER CLOSELY. HER REACTION HAD BEEN TOO QUICK.
HE ADDED HER TO HIS GROWING LIST OF SUSPECTS.

IN POTIONS CLASS, LYLE HOVERED NEAR THE SHELVES, MUTTERING TO HIMSELF. ELLIOT CAUGHT A GLIMPSE OF HIM POCKETING A VIAL. "CAUGHT YOU," ELLIOT THOUGHT, PLANNING TO CONFRONT HIM LATER.

THAT EVENING, ELLIOT FOLLOWED LYLE TO THE PREFECTS' TOWER. INSIDE,
LYLE WAS CAREFULLY MIXING POTIONS. "WHAT ARE YOU DOING?"
ELLIOT DEMANDED, STEPPING INTO THE ROOM.

LYLE SPUN AROUND, HIS FACE PALE. "IT'S NONE OF YOUR BUSINESS," HE SNAPPED, SHOVING THE VIALS INTO A DRAWER. "YOU THINK I STOLE THE POTIONS? I'M JUST TRYING TO HELP!"

ELLIOT HESITATED. "HELP WITH WHAT?" LYLE HESITATED BEFORE BLURTING,
"THEO'S BEEN ACTING STRANGE. I WAS TRYING TO PROTECT THE SCHOOL."

CONFUSED BUT INTRIGUED, ELLIOT LEFT THE TOWER. FELIX TROTTED BESIDE HIM, TAIL FLICKING NERVOUSLY. "WHAT IF THEO REALLY IS BEHIND THIS?" ELLIOT MUTTERED.

THE NEXT DAY, GREGOR CAUGHT ELLIOT SNOOPING NEAR THE GREENHOUSE. "LOOKING FOR TROUBLE, LAD?" GREGOR ASKED, HIS DEEP VOICE ECHOING.

"WHY WOULD I BE?" ELLIOT SAID CASUALLY, THOUGH HIS HEART POUNDED.
HE NOTICED GREGOR'S GLOVES WERE STAINED WITH STRANGE, SHIMMERING LIQUID.

"THAT'S ENOUGH SPYING," GREGOR GROWLED, TOWERING OVER ELLIOT. BUT BEFORE ELLIOT COULD ASK ABOUT THE GLOVES, A BELL RANG, SUMMONING EVERYONE TO THE GREAT HALL.

ELLIOT SAT AT BREAKFAST, STARING AT HIS UNTOUCHED PLATE. HIS MIND CHURNED WITH UNANSWERED QUESTIONS. HEADMISTRESS'S ANNOUNCEMENT ECHOED IN HIS EARS—ALCHEMY LAB CLOSED FOR SAFETY. THIS WASN'T OVER YET.

LATER, ELLIOT CONFRONTED CHARLOTTE IN THE HALLWAY. "YOU'RE HIDING SOMETHING ABOUT THE ELIXIR," HE SAID. SHE STIFFENED. "IT'S DANGEROUS, ELLIOT. DON'T GO DIGGING." BUT HER EYES TOLD HIM THERE WAS MORE.

FRUSTRATED, ELLIOT WATCHED CHARLOTTE WALK AWAY. FELIX RUBBED AGAINST HIS LEG, PURRING. ELLIOT'S GAZE FELL ON A TAPESTRY MOVING SLIGHTLY. HE APPROACHED, DISCOVERING A HIDDEN DOOR. WHAT WAS BEHIND IT?

ELLIOT CREPT THROUGH THE NARROW PASSAGE, HIS HEART POUNDING. THE AIR SMELLED DAMP. THE WINDING STAIRCASE LED HIM TO A GLOWING CHAMBER FILLED WITH FLOATING POTION BOTTLES. SOME FAMILIAR, OTHERS UNFAMILIAR.

SUDDENLY, A LOW GROWL ECHOED. ELLIOT FROZE. SHADOWY FIGURES EMERGED FROM THE DARKNESS—FROST WOLVES, THEIR ICY BLUE EYES GLOWING. HE BACKED UP, HANDS RAISED. "I MEAN NO HARM," HE WHISPERED.

THE WOLVES ADVANCED SLOWLY, THEIR PAWS SILENT ON THE STONE FLOOR. ELLIOT STEPPED BACK. HIS HEART RACED. "I JUST NEED TO FIND OUT WHO'S STEALING THE POTIONS, " HE MUTTERED. FELIX HISSED, BRISTLING.

ELLIOT GLANCED AROUND, LOOKING FOR AN ESCAPE. ONE OF THE WOLVES GROWLED AGAIN.
FELIX, WITH A SUDDEN YOWL, JUMPED ONTO THE STONE ALTAR,
CAUSING A DISTRACTION. THE WOLVES HESITATED FOR A MOMENT.

SEIZING THE CHANCE, ELLIOT BOLTED, RUSHING DOWN THE PASSAGE. HE HEARD THE WOLVES BEHIND HIM, BUT THE PATH GREW NARROWER. HE DUCKED INTO A SMALL ALCOVE, HIDING UNTIL THE DANGER PASSED.

THE WOLVES EVENTUALLY RETREATED, AND ELLIOT SLOWLY EXHALED. "THAT WAS TOO CLOSE," HE MUTTERED, BRUSHING DUST OFF HIS ROBES. FELIX LEAPED ONTO HIS SHOULDER, HIS TAIL TWITCHING NERVOUSLY. SOMETHING STILL WASN'T RIGHT.

ELLIOT MADE HIS WAY BACK TO THE MAIN CORRIDORS, SHAKEN BUT DETERMINED.
HE HAD SEEN ENOUGH TO KNOW SOMEONE HAD A DANGEROUS SECRET. BUT WHO?
AND WHY WERE THE WOLVES GUARDING THE POTIONS?

ELLIOT APPROACHED THE ALCHEMY LAB, HIS MIND RACING. HE HAD TO FIND MORE CLUES BEFORE THE THIEF STRUCK AGAIN. AS HE PEEKED INSIDE, HE NOTICED SOMETHING STRANGE: THE POTION VIAL WAS MISSING AGAIN.

CHARLOTTE'S VOICE BROKE THE SILENCE. "I TOLD YOU TO STAY AWAY, ELLIOT!" SHE STOOD IN THE DOORWAY, EYES WIDE WITH FEAR. "YOU DON'T UNDERSTAND THE DANGER. THEY WILL COME FOR YOU." HER HANDS TREMBLED.

ELLIOT'S EYES NARROWED. "WHO'S AFTER ME, CHARLOTTE? WHAT ARE YOU HIDING?"
SHE SIGHED HEAVILY, STEPPING INTO THE ROOM. "I DIDN'T WANT YOU INVOLVED.
BUT YOU'RE RIGHT. THE POTIONS ARE BEING STOLEN TO CREATE A CURSE."

"A CURSE?" ELLIOT REPEATED, CONFUSED. CHARLOTTE NODDED. "IT'S A POWERFUL SPELL. WHOEVER CONTROLS THE POTION CAN SUMMON THE WOLVES, SPIDERS, EVEN THE KNIGHTS, AND BEND THEM TO THEIR WILL. THAT'S WHAT'S HAPPENING."

ELLIOT'S EYES WIDENED. "THEO? BUT WHY? HE SEEMED…" "NORMAL?"
CHARLOTTE INTERRUPTED BITTERLY. "HE'S BEEN PLAYING EVERYONE, ELLIOT. THE WOLVES, THE
SPIDERS—THEY WERE NEVER SUPPOSED TO BE IN DANGER. IT'S ALL A LIE."

ELLIOT TURNED ON HIS HEEL. "I'M GOING TO STOP HIM." HE RUSHED OUT OF THE LAB, WITH FELIX TRAILING BEHIND HIM. CHARLOTTE'S VOICE CALLED AFTER HIM, BUT HE COULDN'T TURN BACK. THEO HAD TO BE STOPPED.

THE AIR WAS THICK WITH TENSION AS ELLIOT MADE HIS WAY TO THEO'S HIDDEN ROOM.
FELIX HISSED, SENSING THE DANGER. HE KNOCKED ON THE DOOR,
BUT THERE WAS NO ANSWER. THE ROOM FELT COLD, EERILY SILENT.

ELLIOT PUSHED THE DOOR OPEN SLOWLY. THEO STOOD BY A CAULDRON, STIRRING A GLOWING MIXTURE. "I KNEW YOU'D COME," THEO SAID DARKLY. "YOU THINK YOU CAN STOP ME? THE POTION IS ALREADY IN MOTION."

ELLIOT STEPPED FORWARD, A SENSE OF URGENCY BUILDING. "IT'S OVER, THEO. YOU'VE TAKEN ENOUGH FROM THIS SCHOOL." THEO SMIRKED. "NOT YET, ELLIOT. THE MAGIC WILL BE MINE, AND YOU WON'T STOP IT." HE RAISED HIS WAND.

SUDDENLY, THE ROOM SHOOK. WOLVES' HOWLS ECHOED FROM THE HALL. THE GROUND TREMBLED. "YOU'VE GONE TOO FAR, THEO," ELLIOT SHOUTED, RAISING HIS OWN WAND. THE DUEL HAD BEGUN. LIGHTNING CRACKLED BETWEEN THEM.

THEO CAST A BARRAGE OF ICY BOLTS TOWARD ELLIOT. HE DODGED, ROLLING ACROSS THE FLOOR. FELIX LEAPED TO HIS DEFENSE, CLAWING AT THEO'S LEGS. "YOU'RE NOT GOING TO WIN," ELLIOT SHOUTED, NARROWING HIS EYES.

THEO GROWLED IN FRUSTRATION. HE SUMMONED A PACK OF WOLVES TO ATTACK. ELLIOT RAISED HIS WAND, CREATING A SHIELD OF LIGHT. THE WOLVES COLLIDED WITH IT, BUT THEIR ENERGY COULDN'T BREAK THROUGH. HE NEEDED A PLAN.

WITH A FLICK OF HIS WRIST, ELLIOT CONJURED A GUST OF WIND, BLOWING THE WOLVES BACK. BUT THEO WASN'T DONE. HE CHANTED A SPELL, SUMMONING VENOMOUS SPIDERS FROM THE DARK CORNERS OF THE ROOM. ELLIOT'S HEART POUNDED.

THE SPIDERS CRAWLED CLOSER, THEIR EYES GLINTING IN THE DIM LIGHT. ELLIOT LEAPED INTO ACTION, SUMMONING A PROTECTIVE BARRIER AROUND HIMSELF AND FELIX. "THIS ENDS NOW, THEO," HE SHOUTED, CHARGING AT THEO WITH HIS WAND RAISED.

THE DUEL RAGED ON. SPELLS COLLIDED, SENDING SPARKS FLYING. FINALLY, ELLIOT SAW AN OPENING. HE REACHED FOR THE POTION VIAL, STILL GLOWING ON THEO'S TABLE. WITH A SWIFT MOTION, HE SMASHED IT ON THE FLOOR.

THE VIAL SHATTERED, ITS MAGIC SWIRLING INTO THE AIR. THEO STAGGERED BACK, HIS FACE A MASK OF SHOCK AND ANGER. "NO! YOU CAN'T..." HE GASPED, HIS POWER FADING AS THE POTION'S MAGIC VANISHED.

THE WOLVES AND SPIDERS FROZE, THEIR ENCHANTMENT BROKEN. ELLIOT'S WAND GLOWED BRIGHT WITH MAGIC, DISPELLING THE DARK FORCES AROUND THEM. THEO FELL TO HIS KNEES, POWERLESS, AS THE GUARDIANS RETURNED TO THEIR NATURAL FORMS.

"WHY, THEO?" ELLIOT ASKED QUIETLY. THEO'S EYES DARKENED. "I WANTED TO CONTROL EVERYTHING—CONTROL THE POWER OF THE SCHOOL'S MAGIC. BUT I WAS TOO GREEDY. TOO AMBITIOUS." HIS VOICE CRACKED WITH REGRET.

THE HEADMISTRESS ARRIVED, HER FACE STERN. "YOU'VE CAUSED ENOUGH HARM, THEO," SHE SAID. "THE POTION THIEF HAS BEEN CAUGHT. YOU'LL FACE THE CONSEQUENCES OF YOUR ACTIONS." ELLIOT BREATHED A SIGH OF RELIEF.

WITH THEO TAKEN AWAY, ELLIOT AND FELIX RETURNED TO THE ALCHEMY LAB. "YOU DID IT," CHARLOTTE SAID, SMILING SOFTLY. "YOU STOPPED HIM. THE SCHOOL IS SAFE AGAIN." ELLIOT GRINNED, FEELING PROUD BUT EXHAUSTED.

LATER THAT EVENING, ELLIOT WALKED THROUGH THE SCHOOL'S GRAND HALLS, REFLECTING ON EVERYTHING HE'D LEARNED. MAGIC WAS POWERFUL, BUT IT WAS THE CHOICES WE MADE THAT DETERMINED ITS TRUE STRENGTH.

FELIX RUBBED AGAINST HIS LEG, PURRING. ELLIOT KNELT DOWN TO PET HIM, HIS THOUGHTS CLEAR. "WE DID GOOD, FELIX," HE MURMURED. FELIX MEOWED IN AGREEMENT, CURLING UP BESIDE HIM. THE SCHOOL WAS FINALLY AT PEACE.

THE NEXT DAY, THE HEADMISTRESS ADDRESSED THE STUDENTS. "THANKS TO ELLIOT'S BRAVERY, WE'VE STOPPED THE POTION THIEF," SHE SAID. "LET THIS BE A LESSON THAT MAGIC MUST BE USED FOR GOOD, NOT FOR GREED."

ELLIOT SMILED, WATCHING THE STUDENTS CLAP. HE HAD SAVED THE SCHOOL, STOPPED THE THIEF, AND LEARNED A VALUABLE LESSON. WITH FELIX BY HIS SIDE, HE KNEW THAT MORE ADVENTURES AWAITED. BUT FOR NOW, HE WAS JUST HAPPY.

I HOPE YOU LIKED THE BOOK. PLEASE FIND OUT OTHER BOOKS BY ME.

www.ingramcontent.com/pod-product-compliance
Lightning Source LLC
Chambersburg PA
CBHW081107300726
48976CB00010B/2686